TEENAGE MUTANT NINJA TURTLES®

A FISHY ADVENTURE

Illustrated by the GEE Studio

Adapted from a story by
Dean Clarrain and Ryan Brown
Based on the Teenage Mutant Ninja Turtles
characters and comic book created by
Kevin Eastman and Peter Laird

RANDOM HOUSE
Happy House Group

"Greetings! I'm Leonardo, one of the Teenage Mutant Ninja Turtle team of fair-fighting reptiles. We turtles are always battling something. But whether it's the Shredder or Krang or Bebop and Rocksteady that we're fighting, we never take advantage of our opponents. However, the other turtles and I recently had an encounter with a torpedo that wanted to take advantage of us! We'd let our guard down, and the Shredder almost turned us into soup! He would have succeeded, too, if it weren't for the help of someone new—a peaceful stranger who had the opportunity to defeat the Shredder..."

"Gosh!" said Donatello.

"Wow!" said Leonardo.

"Whee!" said Raphael.

"Like, what a totally rad fish!" said Michaelangelo.

The four Teenage Mutant Ninja Turtles were standing in front of a large aquarium tank early one summer evening. Just then the curator of the aquarium approached.

"Excuse me, but that's not a fish," the curator, Jack Finney, said. "See the fins on its head? It's called the giant devil ray, or the manta ray. Rays are found in the Atlantic Ocean, near the water's surface. Sometimes they even leap clear out of the water!" He wiggled his fingers above his head, as though he had fins too. "Manta rays are full of grace and joy. I only hope that coastal pollution doesn't do them in."

By the time the turtles left the aquarium it was already dark.

"Hey, let's follow the shore back to the city," suggested Raphael.

"Good thing there's a full moon out—it'll be a long hike," said Leonardo.

"So let's get some pizza real soon!" said Michaelangelo. "Seeing all those fish made me hungry!"

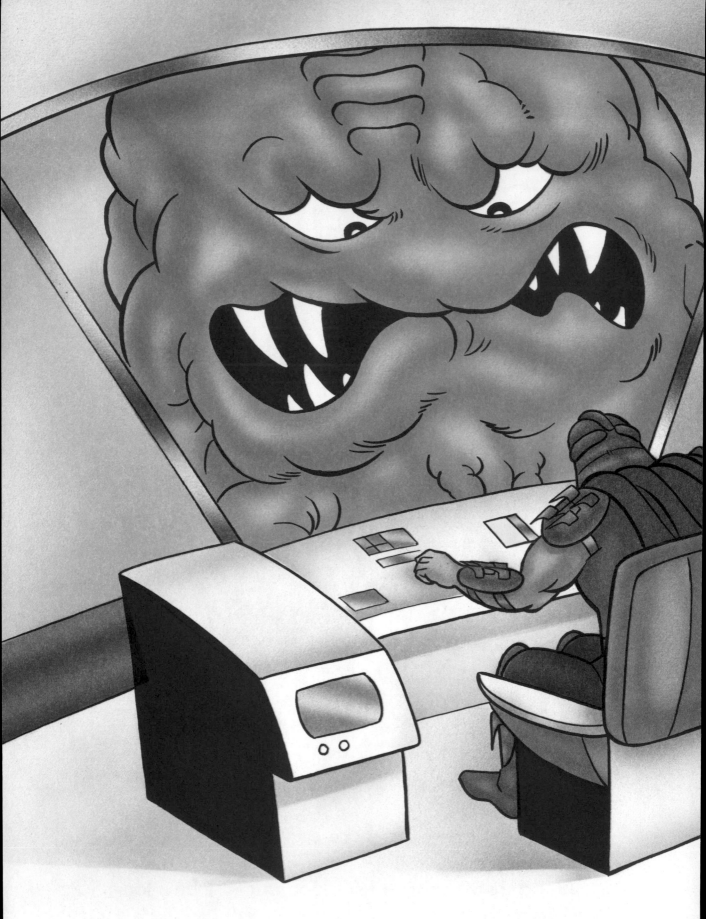

Meanwhile, the brain creature Krang was arguing with the evil Shredder, who sat in his secret submarine in the city's harbor.

"What do you mean you spilled a barrel of mutagen into a sewer?" Krang bellowed from the communicator screen. "Don't you know how rare it is?"

"But Krang," protested Shredder, "it wasn't my fault. Bebop and Rocksteady did it!"

The two mutant punks stopped mopping the deck and looked at each other nervously.

"Well, punish them then," Krang said. "Now, let me tell you about my plans for tonight. I'm going to make it a Fourth of July people will never forget!"

Later that evening, Jack Finney said good night to the huge manta ray. "You're so friendly," he said, reaching into the tank and patting it gently. "I'll see you tomorrow."

Then he closed the aquarium, locked the door, and quickly walked to his car.

"Now for some *real* work!" he said with a grin.

Jack drove to Bayview Beach and parked near a large sewer pipe—a pipe that he suspected was being used for illegal dumping. He dipped his fingers in the liquid coming out of the pipe.

A strange glowing gel clung to his hand!

"I'd better get some samples," Jack said, climbing into the pipe itself. "I guess I should have worn gloves—"

Rumble! "What's that?" the curator wondered.

Whoooosh! A wave of mutagen flooded out of the pipe and carried Jack off.

"Yikes!" he yelled—but there was no one to hear him. And there was no one to see him pulled down into the murky depths of the water—and transformed...

Meanwhile, the four turtles had made their way through marshy reeds and arrived on the beach. They playfully scuffled with one another until Leonardo suddenly said, "Take a break, brothers—it feels like we're being watched."

Leonardo was right. Bebop and Rocksteady were watching the turtles through the submarine periscope. The two mutants ran to report their findings to Shredder right away.

"How convenient!" sneered Shredder. "Once the turtles are out of the way, I can proceed with my plans to destroy the Statue of Liberty! Rocksteady, aim a torpedo at the beach—and when I give the word, fire!"

Little did Shredder and the mutant punks know, but a mysterious creature beneath the sub had overheard everything.

Rocksteady readied the torpedo. Then Shredder gave
the order to fire.

Swoosh! The torpedo zoomed across the water
toward the beach.

The turtles spotted the torpedo coming straight at
them. But before it could reach them, something
suddenly swooped around the missile from underwater
and pulled it back below!

"What was *that?*" asked Leonardo.

Back in the sub, Bebop looked through the periscope. What should he see but the torpedo, coming back to the sub!

"Idiot! Raise the sub now!" Shredder screamed.

Bwaang! The torpedo struck the sub and bounced off, making a dent in the side.

"Get us back to base immediately!" Shredder yelled.

Back on the beach the Teenage Mutant Ninja Turtles looked at one another with relief.

"We could have been killed!" said Raphael.

"What do you make of it, Leonardo?" asked Donatello.

"Well, there's no way we can catch whoever fired the torpedo," Leonardo said. "Still, I wonder what stopped it."

Michaelangelo smiled. "I bet we have a guardian angelfish!" he said.

"Let's follow the sewers back to the city and see what we can find out," Leonardo suggested.

A short while later at the Shredder's secret pier beneath the city, Shredder examined his sub.

"Good! There's no damage," he said. He turned to Bebop and Rocksteady. "Come along. Help me carry the proper explosives from the storage area to the sub. And you'd better not drop anything!"

Unknown to Shredder, the mysterious creature who had turned the torpedo around was now attaching plastic explosives to the underside of the sub.

Elsewhere in the sewers the turtles were slogging through chest-high water. Leonardo led the way.

Suddenly the water surface rippled as something huge moved below. "Quick! Spread out!" shouted Raphael.

The foursome jumped onto a ledge as the unseen Ray Fillet passed by.

"Weird!" said Leonardo, Raphael, and Michaelangelo.

"Something fishy's going on around here, for sure!" Donatello said grimly.

Leonardo pointed down the sewer. "Hey, look—there's a light at the end of the tunnel!"

With a *whoosh* the four turtles splashed down from the sewer-tunnel ledge and landed next to the Shredder's pier.

"Well, what do you know!" Leonardo said, looking at the submarine sitting in the water. "Shall we stow away and see what's going down?"

"Cool!" Michaelangelo said with a grin.

On the shore of the city's harbor the giant figure of Ray Fillet—once Jack Finney—stood quietly. "Lost track of time..." he muttered. "Late...moonlight...so bright...almost hate to do what must be done...plastic explosives attached to sub... will detonate with harpoon ...in harbor away from city ...must save people..."

He dived into the harbor. "Must save water...must save Statue of Liberty!"

Ray Fillet swam underwater out into the harbor.
Picking up a harpoon gun that was lying on a sunken
wrecked car, he aimed it toward the Shredder's sub in
the distance.

Then Ray Fillet saw a face peering through a porthole. It was Michaelangelo.

"I can't see a thing," Michaelangelo complained, turning to his friends. "But we're definitely in deep water."

"Hey, you guys!" shouted Rocksteady. The turtles turned to see Rocksteady and Bebop ready for a fight.

"Chill out, you boneheads!" shouted Donatello, smashing into the mutants with a *whomp!* Rocksteady crashed against the hull's wall—

and ocean water came bursting through!

"Nice going!" Leonardo said sarcastically as he and the others jumped back from the rush of water.

Elsewhere in the submarine, Shredder waded toward the hatch. "A good leader knows when to quit," he said to himself. "With my new air tank and submersible, I'll make it back to base in no time!"

He swam out the hatch. "Sink or swim, fools!"

Bebop and Rocksteady looked out a porthole at the departing Shredder. "Mister Shredder, don't leave us here!" they called after him.

Donatello and Raphael sneaked up behind the mutant punks. *Shoonk! Shoonk!* They flung life preservers over the punks' heads, pinning their arms to their sides.

As the turtles, Bebop, and Rocksteady bobbed up to the surface the sub slowly sank to the ocean floor.

The punks twisted uncomfortably in their preservers. "How humiliating!" Bebop whined.

"Uh, Bebop, are there, like, sharks around here?" Rocksteady asked nervously.

"Hey, you guys!" both punks called to the turtles. "Help us!" But the turtles were already swimming away.

"Keep on going, Raphael," said Donatello. "Liberty Island's not far!"

Meanwhile, Shredder was busy swimming too. He laughed evilly to himself, thinking how easily he had escaped the sinking sub.

Suddenly something loomed up in front of him.

"Huh? What's that?" Shredder said. startled.

It was Ray Fillet, strong and defiant.

"I am the end...to your twisted plans, evil one!" he said menacingly. "I am...Ray Fillet!"

Shredder gulped. Then he tossed away his submersible. "Ray Fillet? It was you who turned the torpedo back on my sub! And saved those annoying turtles!" He lunged toward the creature. "Here's one for you, monster!"

"You—you are the monster!" Ray Fillet growled.

Whomp! Shredder's fist connected with Ray Fillet's shoulder. The harpoon went flying.

Rip! Rip! Ray Fillet disconnected Shredder's air hoses.

"Glub! Glub!" Shredder could barely breathe. Ray Fillet grabbed the Shredder's cape and towed him to the water's surface.

"Must get back…to water…to rest," Ray Fillet said in exhaustion as he slowly dragged Shredder onto the shore of Liberty Island.

The half-man, half-ray creature paused, and Shredder saw his chance. With one smooth motion he kicked a flurry of sand into Ray Fillet's face.

Then, with an evil laugh, the Shredder turned and ran, shouting, "To your fate, fool!"

"Hey, dude, are you all right?" Leonardo called anxiously. The turtles hurried over to their newfound friend.

Ray Fillet got to his feet. "Shredder planned...to destroy liberty statue...ruin fireworks celebration... tonight," he said, gasping for breath. "But new body... difficult to speak...I must return to water...."

"Go in peace, friend," Leonardo said as Ray Fillet
dived into the water.

"And thank you!" the others called.

"Wonder what his story is," Donatello said.

"He looks like that aquarium manta ray,"
Michaelangelo said. "Like some sort of manta man."

"Well, whoever he is, he helped us put an end to the
Shredder's plans," said Raphael.

"At least for now!" added Leonardo as spectacular
fireworks began to explode in the night sky behind
them.